The Littlest
Christmas Tree

Text copyright © 2007 by R.A. Herman.
Illustrations copyright © 2007 by Jacqueline Rogers.
All rights reserved. Published by Scholastic Inc.

SCHOLASTIC, CARTWHEEL BOOKS, and associated logos are
trademarks and/or registered trademarks of Scholastic Inc.

Library of Congress Cataloging-in-Publication Data
Herman, R. A. (Ronnie Ann)
The littlest Christmas tree / by R.A. Herman ; illustrated by
Jacqueline Rogers.
p. cm. -- "Cartwheel books."
Summary: As the holiday approaches and all the larger trees on the lot
are chosen, the Littlest Tree becomes resigned to not finding a home for Christmas.
ISBN-13: 978-0-439-54007-0 (pbk.)
ISBN-10: 0-439-54007-0 (pbk.)
[1. Christmas trees--Fiction. 2. Christmas--Fiction. 3. Size--Fiction.]
I. Rogers, Jacqueline, ill. II. Title.
PZ7.H43155Lic 2007
[E]--dc22   2006026254

ISBN-13: 978-0-439-54007-0
ISBN-10: 0-439-54007-0

12 11 10 9 8 7 6 5   08   14 15 16 17 18/0

Printed in the U.S.A.
First printing, October 2007

The Littlest Christmas Tree

by R.A. Herman
Illustrated by Jacqueline Rogers

Cartwheel
B·O·O·K·S ®

SCHOLASTIC INC.
New York Toronto London Auckland Sydney
Mexico City New Delhi Hong Kong Buenos Aires

It was December 20, only five days until Christmas, and the Littlest Tree was at a Christmas tree stand on the main street of town.

There were all different kinds of evergreen trees
at the stand: spruce, firs, and pines.

The trees were all different sizes and shapes: tall, thin, fat, and short, but the Littlest Tree was certainly the smallest.

The Littlest Tree had a big wish. "I wish that someone would take me home this Christmas and make me beautiful with decorations. Then everyone would gather around me to sing my favorite Christmas carol. *Oh, Christmas tree, oh, Christmas tree, how lovely are thy branches* . . . I can't wait to be a Christmas tree."

On that beautiful winter day, when the sky was bright blue
and there wasn't a cloud to be seen, Gabriel and Simone came
to the Christmas tree stand with their mom and dad.

"Oh, I want this one!" cried Gabriel, running right up to the Biggest Fir Tree.

Simone said, "*Twee!*"

"See," said Gabriel, "Simone wants this one, too!"

"Oh, no," said Mom. "This one is too tall. We would need to put a hole in our ceiling for it to fit in our house."

When the Littlest Tree heard this, it thought, "Maybe they will want *me* to be their Christmas tree if the fir tree is too big. I could easily fit into their house."

But the family looked at all the other trees without even glancing at the Littlest Tree. They studied and measured each one until they found the perfect tree.

Early the next morning, when there was still some frost on the trees, an old man and woman walked by the stand. The Littlest Tree stood up as tall as it could, shook out its needles, and tried to look its very best.

As they looked at the Littlest Tree, the old man said, "This one is small enough for us to carry home ourselves."

"Isn't it sweet?" said the old woman. But just then, they noticed the Biggest Tree standing up tall and said, "What a beautiful tree. This tree must be older than you and me combined." And they asked the man at the stand to carry it to their house.

The next day was freezing cold, and all the trees' branches were blowing in the wind. Twin brothers came to the stand with their grandma and grandpa.

"Let's pick a tree quickly. It is freezing!" said Grandpa. "Then we can go have some hot chocolate and warm up."

They chose a tall, skinny tree and ran shivering to their car with it, and drove away.

All the next day, people came to the stand to find their perfect Christmas trees. Many people looked at the Littlest Tree and said that it was cute, but no one took it home.

Finally, Christmas Eve arrived. The Littlest Tree thought, "Oh, dear, tomorrow is Christmas, and I *so* want to be a Christmas tree. If no one chooses me today, then my wish will never come true." The Littlest Tree opened its branches as wide as possible and tried hard to be seen.

Very few people came to the stand that day.
Most people were home baking cookies,

wrapping presents,

and decorating their
Christmas trees.

The Littlest Tree tried singing to cheer itself up. *"On the first day of Christmas, my true love gave to me a partridge in a pear tree.* I am not a pear tree, and I'm not a Christmas tree yet, either."

There were hardly any trees left, and the sky was getting dark quickly. Soon the streetlights came on. A few snowflakes began to fall and started to stick to the Littlest Tree's branches.

The Littlest Tree felt quite beautiful with the snowflakes decorating it. A little icicle formed from one of its branches as the Littlest Tree began to cry. It felt lonely.

The man was getting ready to close up his stand for the
night. He wanted to get home to celebrate Christmas Eve
with his family. He still had a lot of presents to wrap.

As he was leaving, he glanced at the Littlest Tree. He picked it up and put it under his arm. "Where is he taking me?" the Littlest Tree wondered.

They walked for what seemed like forever, and then suddenly stopped. The man carried the Littlest Tree inside, where it was warm and smelled of yummy things. The Littlest Tree looked around and thought, "Oh, this must be a home."

A little boy and a woman ran up to the man and kissed him. "Merry Christmas!" they cried, and the man handed the Littlest Tree to the boy.

"I thought this was the perfect tree for you, Nathan. You can put it in your room and have your very own Christmas tree."

Nathan took the Littlest Tree into his bedroom and found the perfect place for it to stand. The Littlest Tree stood up as tall as it could.

Nathan's mom and dad cooked popcorn and helped Nathan
string the popcorn with cranberries to make garlands. They cut
out snowflakes and stars from white paper. Then they made a
big star from silver foil for the topmost branch.

They strung tiny twinkling lights on the Littlest Tree, and Nathan decorated it with everything they had made. He even put presents under the tree. The Littlest Tree was so excited, it felt ten feet tall.

"Oh, what a perfect Christmas tree!" said Nathan. They all gathered around the Littlest Christmas Tree and sang, "*Oh, Christmas tree, oh, Christmas tree, how lovely are thy branches . . .*"

"I am now a Christmas tree!" thought the Littlest Tree.
And it was the loveliest and happiest Christmas tree in the
whole world that Christmas, when all its wishes came true.